TEENAGE MUTANT NINJA TURTLES

DONATELLO

Story by **Brian Lynch**
Script by **Brian Lynch** and **Tom Waltz**
Artwork by **Valerio Schiti**
Colors by **ScarletGothica** and **Ilaria Traversi**
Lettering by **Robbie Robbins**

 Spotlight

ABDOPUBLISHING.COM

Reinforced library bound edition published in 2015 by Spotlight,
a division of ABDO, PO Box 398166, Minneapolis, Minnesota 55439.
Spotlight produces high-quality reinforced library bound editions for
schools and libraries. Published by agreement with IDW.

Printed in the United States of America, North Mankato, Minnesota.
112014
012015

THIS BOOK CONTAINS
RECYCLED MATERIALS

LIBRARY OF CONGRESS CATALOGING-IN-PUBLICATION DATA

Lynch, Brian (Brian Michael), 1973- author.
 Donatello / writers, Brian Lynch and Tom Waltz ; artist, Valerio Schiti. --
Reinforced library bound edition.
     pages cm. -- (Teenage Mutant Ninja Turtles)
 Summary: Donatello goes incognito to a science fair and finds out that it's
being put on by none other than Baxter Stockman"-- Provided by publisher.
 ISBN 978-1-61479-338-0
1. Graphic novels. I. Waltz, Tom, author. II. Schiti, Valerio, illustrator. III.
Teenage Mutant Ninja Turtles (Television program : 2012-) IV. Title.
 PZ7.7.L95Do 2015
 741.5'973--dc23

                    2014038214

Spotlight

A Division of ABDO
abdopublishing.com

I'M DONATELLO TEENAGE MUTANT NINJA TURTLE

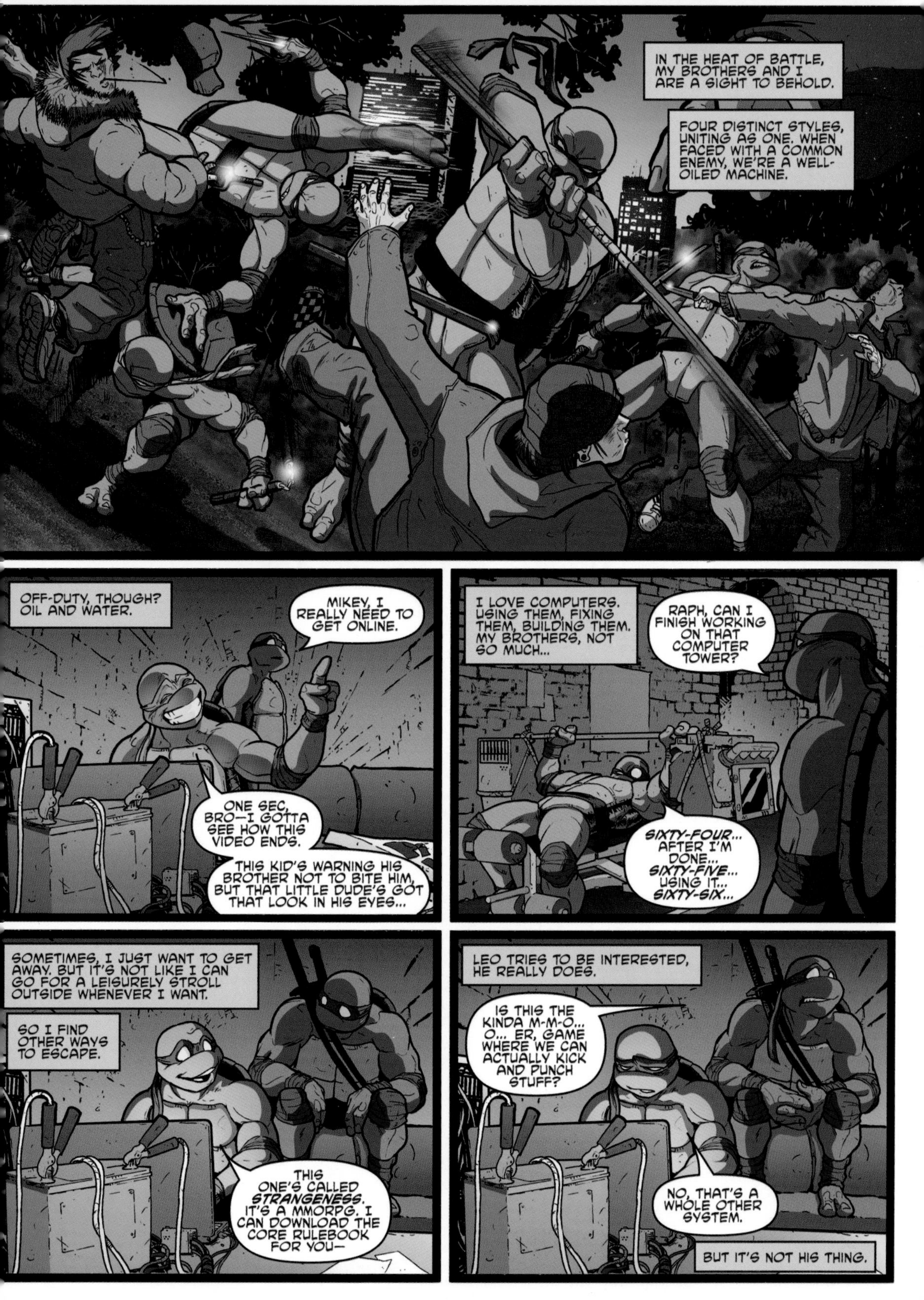

IN THE HEAT OF BATTLE, MY BROTHERS AND I ARE A SIGHT TO BEHOLD.
FOUR DISTINCT STYLES, UNITING AS ONE. WHEN FACED WITH A COMMON ENEMY, WE'RE A WELL-OILED MACHINE.
OFF-DUTY, THOUGH? OIL AND WATER.
MIKEY, I REALLY NEED TO GET ONLINE.
ONE SEC, BRO—I GOTTA SEE HOW THIS VIDEO ENDS.
THIS KID'S WARNING HIS BROTHER NOT TO BITE HIM, BUT THAT LITTLE DUDE'S GOT THAT LOOK IN HIS EYES...
I LOVE COMPUTERS. USING THEM, FIXING THEM, BUILDING THEM. MY BROTHERS, NOT SO MUCH...
RAPH, CAN I FINISH WORKING ON THAT COMPUTER TOWER?
SIXTY-FOUR... AFTER I'M DONE... SIXTY-FIVE... USING IT... SIXTY-SIX...
SOMETIMES, I JUST WANT TO GET AWAY. BUT IT'S NOT LIKE I CAN GO FOR A LEISURELY STROLL OUTSIDE WHENEVER I WANT.
SO I FIND OTHER WAYS TO ESCAPE.
THIS ONE'S CALLED STRANGENESS. IT'S A MMORPG. I CAN DOWNLOAD THE CORE RULEBOOK FOR YOU—
LEO TRIES TO BE INTERESTED, HE REALLY DOES.
IS THIS THE KINDA M-M-O... O... ER, GAME WHERE WE CAN ACTUALLY KICK AND PUNCH STUFF?
NO, THAT'S A WHOLE OTHER SYSTEM.
BUT IT'S NOT HIS THING.

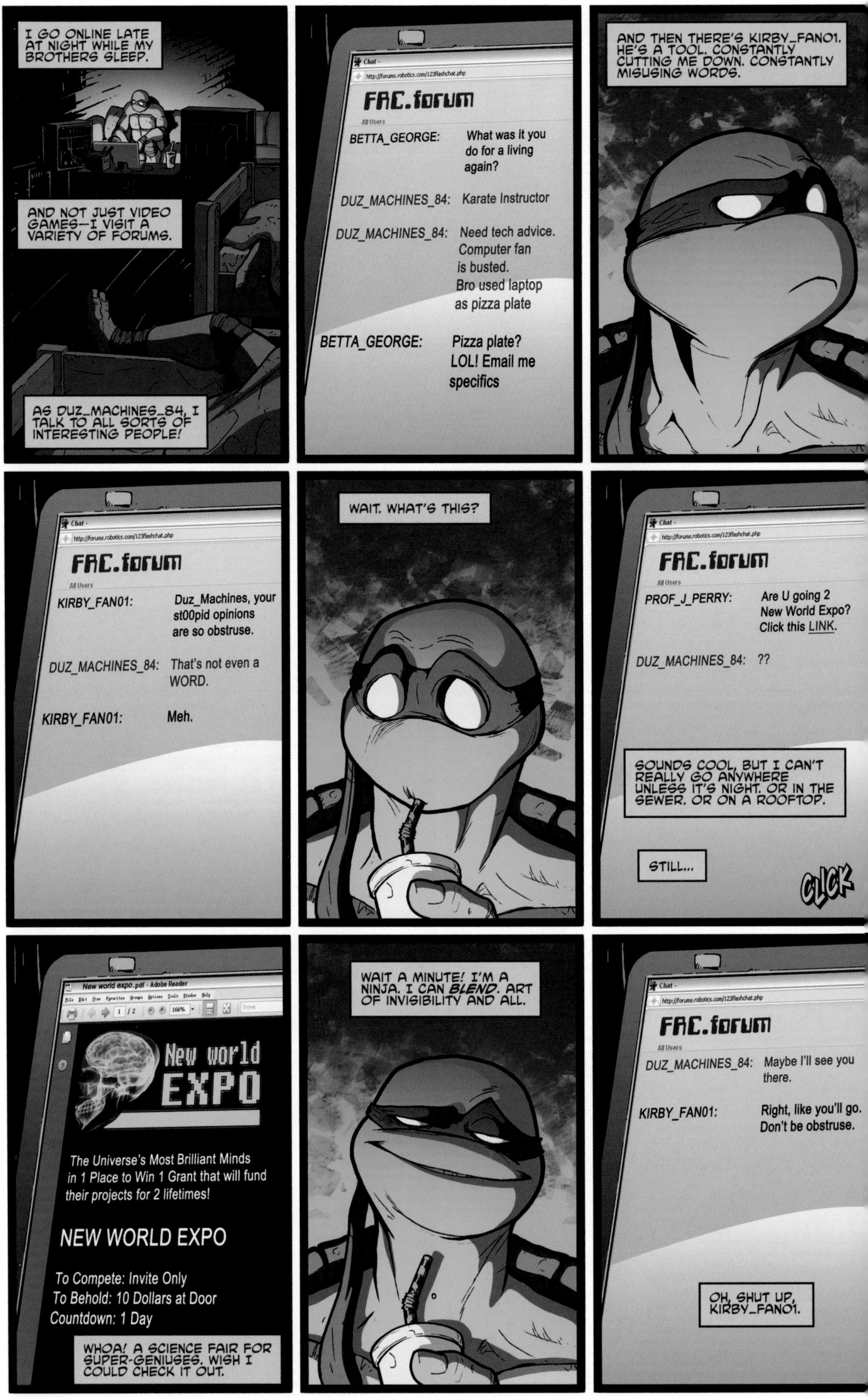

I GO ONLINE LATE AT NIGHT WHILE MY BROTHERS SLEEP.
AND NOT JUST VIDEO GAMES—I VISIT A VARIETY OF FORUMS.
AS DUZ_MACHINES_84, I TALK TO ALL SORTS OF INTERESTING PEOPLE!
Chat -
http://forums.robotics.com/123flashchat.php
FRC.forum
All Users
BETTA_GEORGE: What was it you do for a living again?
DUZ_MACHINES_84: Karate Instructor
DUZ_MACHINES_84: Need tech advice. Computer fan is busted. Bro used laptop as pizza plate
BETTA_GEORGE: Pizza plate? LOL! Email me specifics
AND THEN THERE'S KIRBY_FAN01. HE'S A TOOL. CONSTANTLY CUTTING ME DOWN. CONSTANTLY MISUSING WORDS.
Chat -
http://forums.robotics.com/123flashchat.php
FRC.forum
All Users
KIRBY_FAN01: Duz_Machines, your st00pid opinions are so obstruse.
DUZ_MACHINES_84: That's not even a WORD.
KIRBY_FAN01: Meh.
WAIT. WHAT'S THIS?
Chat -
http://forums.robotics.com/123flashchat.php
FRC.forum
All Users
PROF_J_PERRY: Are U going 2 New World Expo? Click this LINK.
DUZ_MACHINES_84: ??
SOUNDS COOL, BUT I CAN'T REALLY GO ANYWHERE UNLESS IT'S NIGHT. OR IN THE SEWER. OR ON A ROOFTOP.
STILL...
CLICK
New world expo.pdf - Adobe Reader
New world EXPO
The Universe's Most Brilliant Minds in 1 Place to Win 1 Grant that will fund their projects for 2 lifetimes!
NEW WORLD EXPO
To Compete: Invite Only
To Behold: 10 Dollars at Door
Countdown: 1 Day
WHOA! A SCIENCE FAIR FOR SUPER-GENIUSES. WISH I COULD CHECK IT OUT.
WAIT A MINUTE! I'M A NINJA. I CAN *BLEND*. ART OF INVISIBILITY AND ALL.
Chat -
http://forums.robotics.com/123flashchat.php
FRC.forum
All Users
DUZ_MACHINES_84: Maybe I'll see you there.
KIRBY_FAN01: Right, like you'll go. Don't be obstruse.
OH, SHUT UP, KIRBY_FAN01.

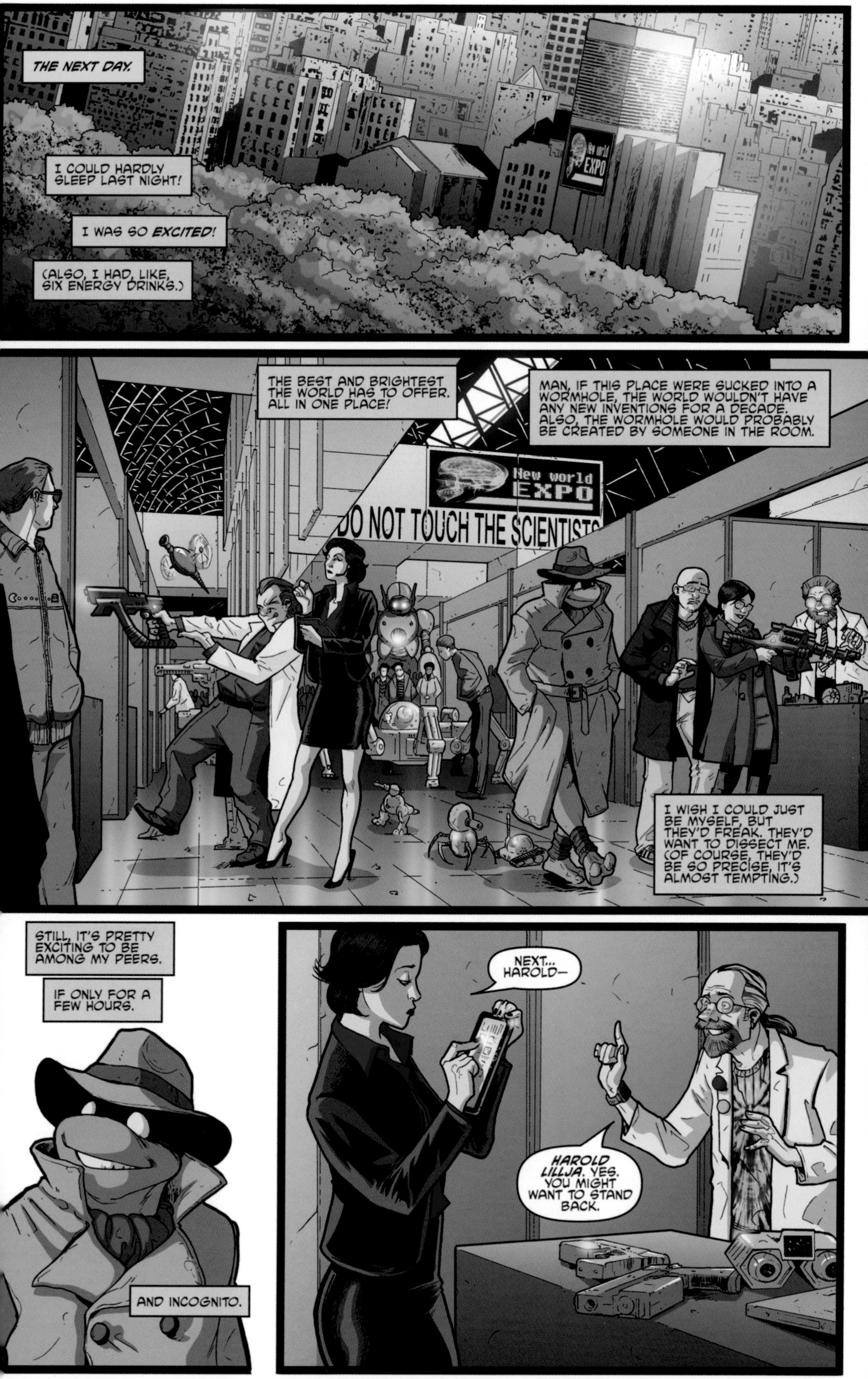
THE NEXT DAY.
I COULD HARDLY SLEEP LAST NIGHT!
I WAS SO EXCITED!
(ALSO, I HAD, LIKE, SIX ENERGY DRINKS.)
New world EXPO
THE BEST AND BRIGHTEST THE WORLD HAS TO OFFER. ALL IN ONE PLACE!
MAN, IF THIS PLACE WERE SUCKED INTO A WORMHOLE, THE WORLD WOULDN'T HAVE ANY NEW INVENTIONS FOR A DECADE. ALSO, THE WORMHOLE WOULD PROBABLY BE CREATED BY SOMEONE IN THE ROOM.
New world EXPO
DO NOT TOUCH THE SCIENTISTS
I WISH I COULD JUST BE MYSELF, BUT THEY'D FREAK. THEY'D WANT TO DISSECT ME. (OF COURSE, THEY'D BE SO PRECISE, IT'S ALMOST TEMPTING.)
STILL, IT'S PRETTY EXCITING TO BE AMONG MY PEERS.
IF ONLY FOR A FEW HOURS.
AND INCOGNITO.
NEXT... HAROLD—
HAROLD LILLJA. YES. YOU MIGHT WANT TO STAND BACK.

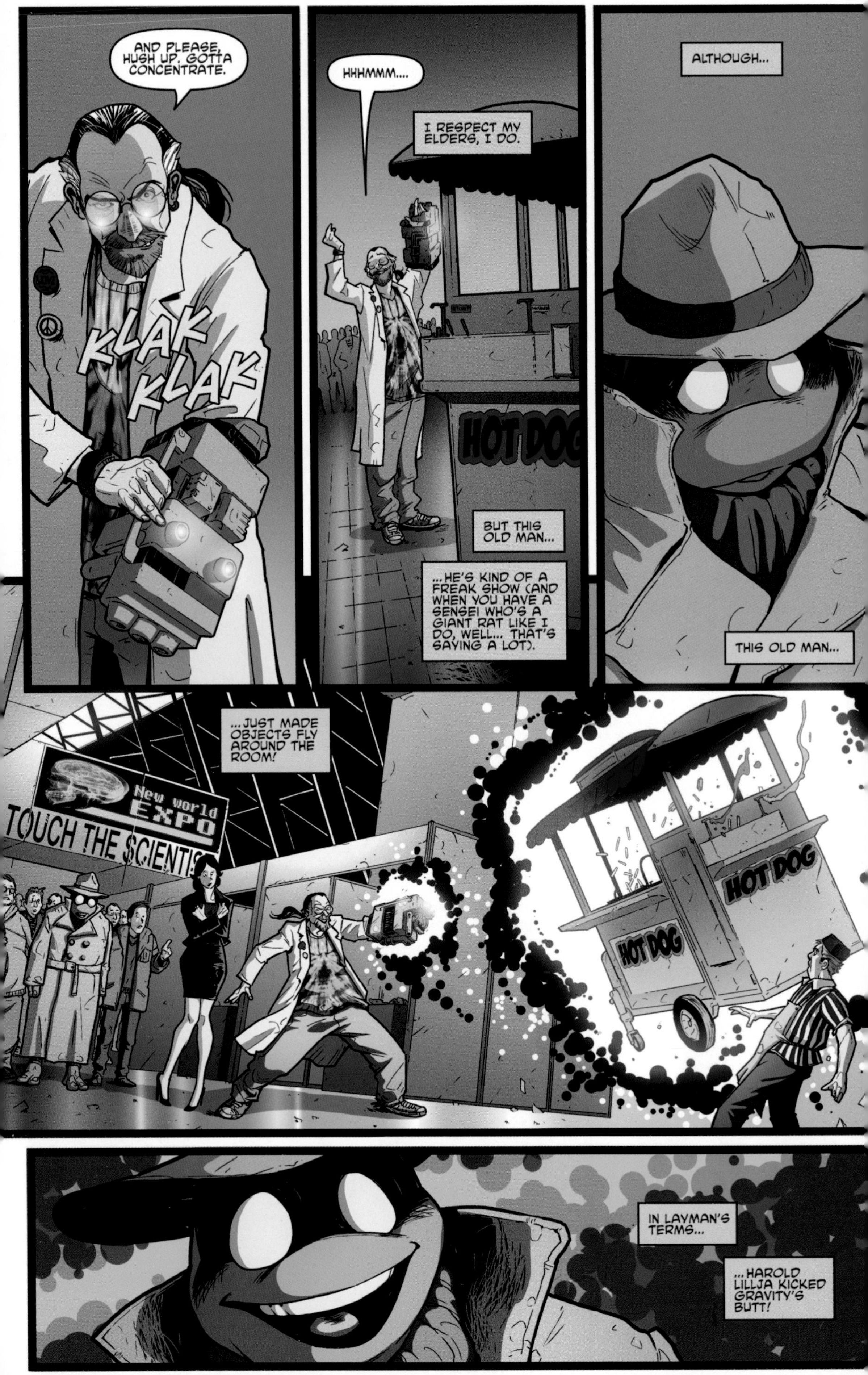
AND PLEASE, HUSH UP. GOTTA CONCENTRATE.
KLAK KLAK
HHHMMM....
I RESPECT MY ELDERS, I DO.
HOT DOG
BUT THIS OLD MAN...
...HE'S KIND OF A FREAK SHOW (AND WHEN YOU HAVE A SENSEI WHO'S A GIANT RAT LIKE I DO, WELL... THAT'S SAYING A LOT).
ALTHOUGH...
THIS OLD MAN...
...JUST MADE OBJECTS FLY AROUND THE ROOM!
New world EXPO
TOUCH THE SCIENTIS
HOT DOG
HOT DOG
IN LAYMAN'S TERMS...
...HAROLD LILLJA KICKED GRAVITY'S BUTT!

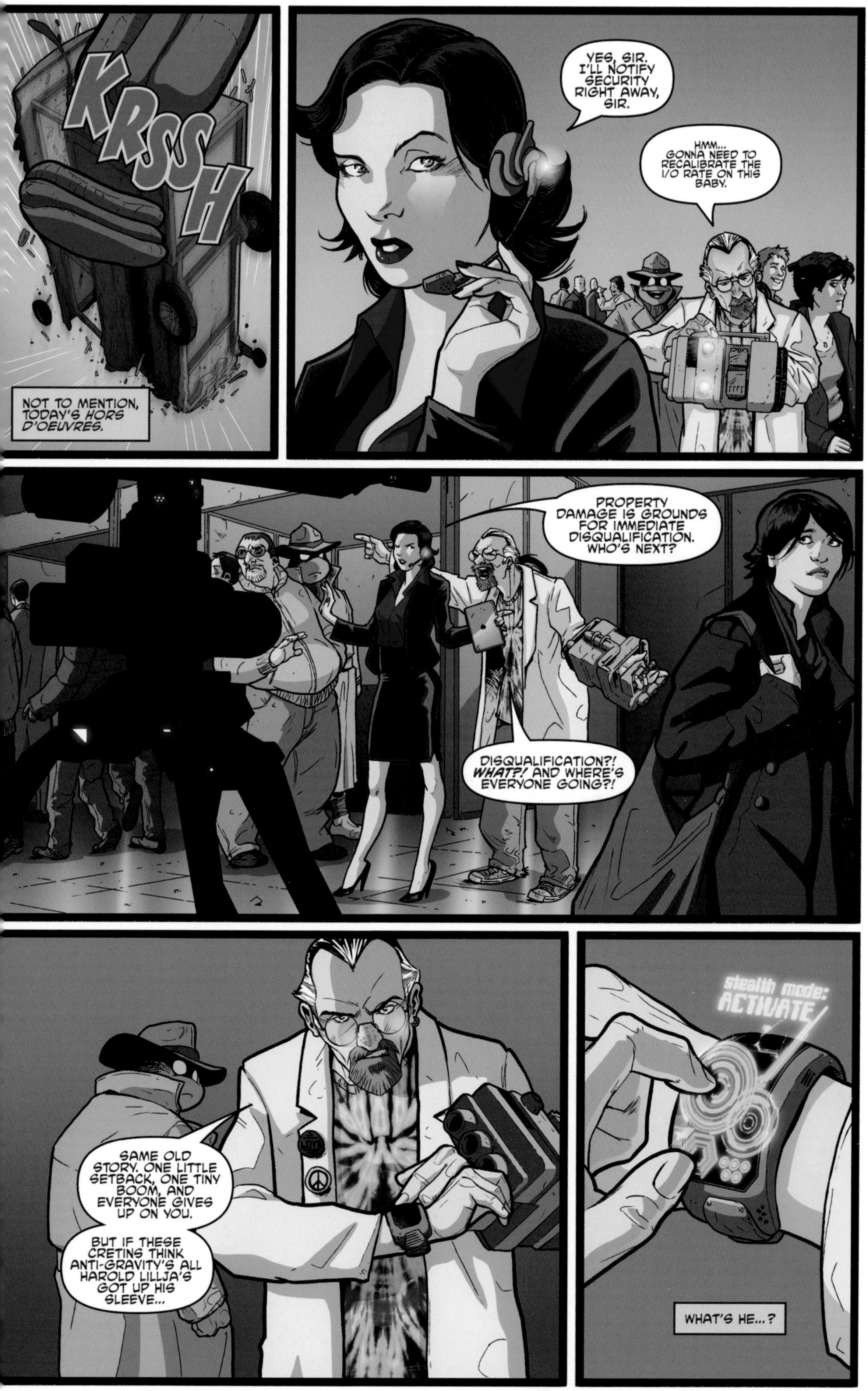
KRSSH
NOT TO MENTION, TODAY'S *HORS D'OEUVRES.*
YES, SIR. I'LL NOTIFY SECURITY RIGHT AWAY, SIR.
HMM... GONNA NEED TO RECALIBRATE THE I/O RATE ON THIS BABY.
PROPERTY DAMAGE IS GROUNDS FOR IMMEDIATE DISQUALIFICATION. WHO'S NEXT?
DISQUALIFICATION?! *WHAT?!* AND WHERE'S EVERYONE GOING?!
SAME OLD STORY. ONE LITTLE SETBACK, ONE TINY BOOM, AND EVERYONE GIVES UP ON YOU.
BUT IF THESE CRETINS THINK ANTI-GRAVITY'S ALL HAROLD LILLJA'S GOT UP HIS SLEEVE...
stealth mode: ACTIVATE
WHAT'S HE...?

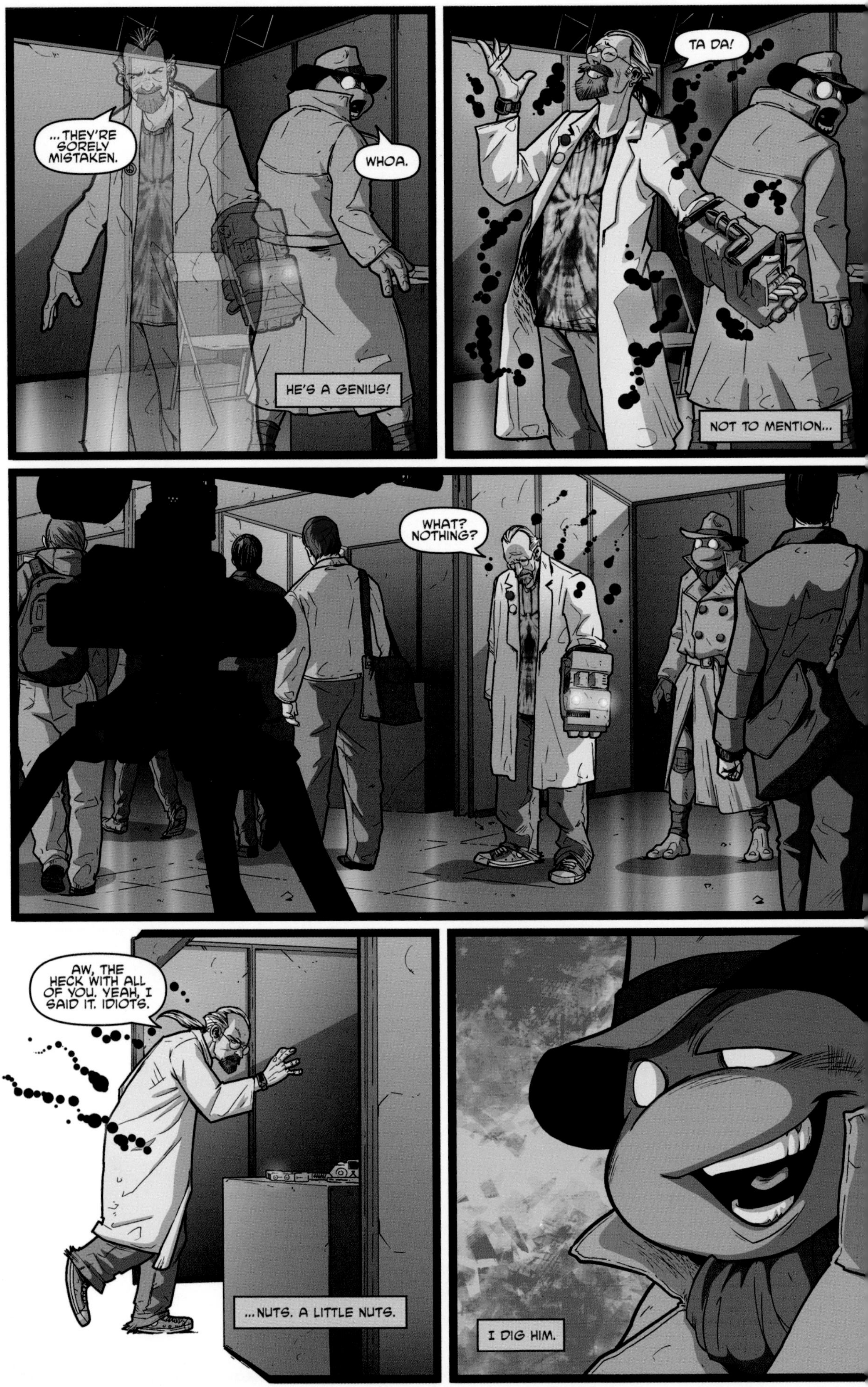
...THEY'RE SORELY MISTAKEN.
WHOA.
HE'S A GENIUS!
TA DA!
NOT TO MENTION...
WHAT? NOTHING?
AW, THE HECK WITH ALL OF YOU. YEAH, I SAID IT. IDIOTS.
...NUTS. A LITTLE NUTS.
I DIG HIM.

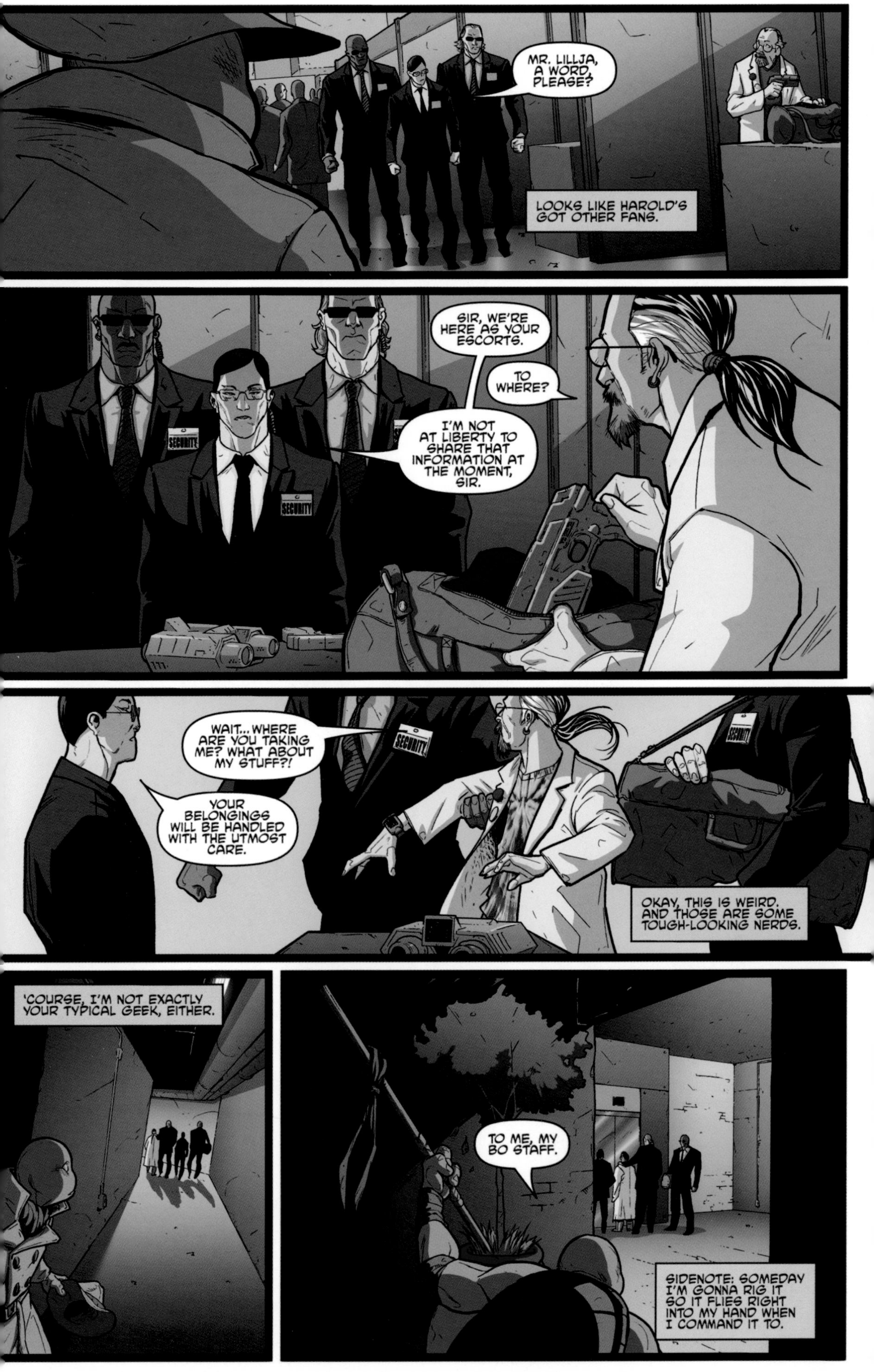
MR. LILLJA, A WORD, PLEASE?
LOOKS LIKE HAROLD'S GOT OTHER FANS.
SIR, WE'RE HERE AS YOUR ESCORTS.
TO WHERE?
I'M NOT AT LIBERTY TO SHARE THAT INFORMATION AT THE MOMENT, SIR.
SECURITY
SECURITY
WAIT... WHERE ARE YOU TAKING ME? WHAT ABOUT MY STUFF?!
YOUR BELONGINGS WILL BE HANDLED WITH THE UTMOST CARE.
SECURITY
SECURITY
OKAY, THIS IS WEIRD. AND THOSE ARE SOME TOUGH-LOOKING NERDS.
'COURSE, I'M NOT EXACTLY YOUR TYPICAL GEEK, EITHER.
TO ME, MY BO STAFF.
SIDENOTE: SOMEDAY I'M GONNA RIG IT SO IT FLIES RIGHT INTO MY HAND WHEN I COMMAND IT TO.

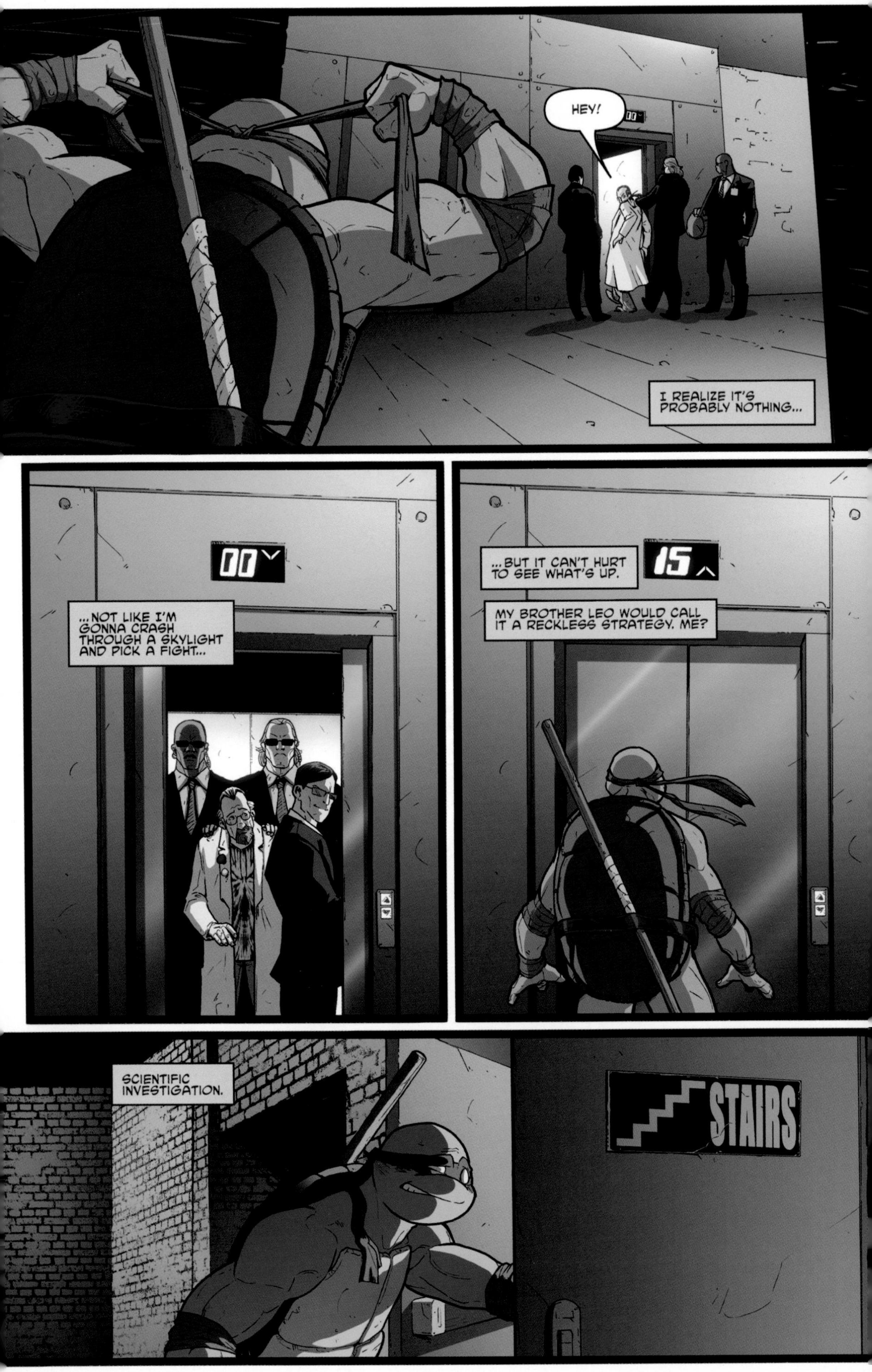
HEY!
00
I REALIZE IT'S PROBABLY NOTHING...
00
...NOT LIKE I'M GONNA CRASH THROUGH A SKYLIGHT AND PICK A FIGHT...
...BUT IT CAN'T HURT TO SEE WHAT'S UP.
15
MY BROTHER LEO WOULD CALL IT A RECKLESS STRATEGY. ME?
SCIENTIFIC INVESTIGATION.
STAIRS

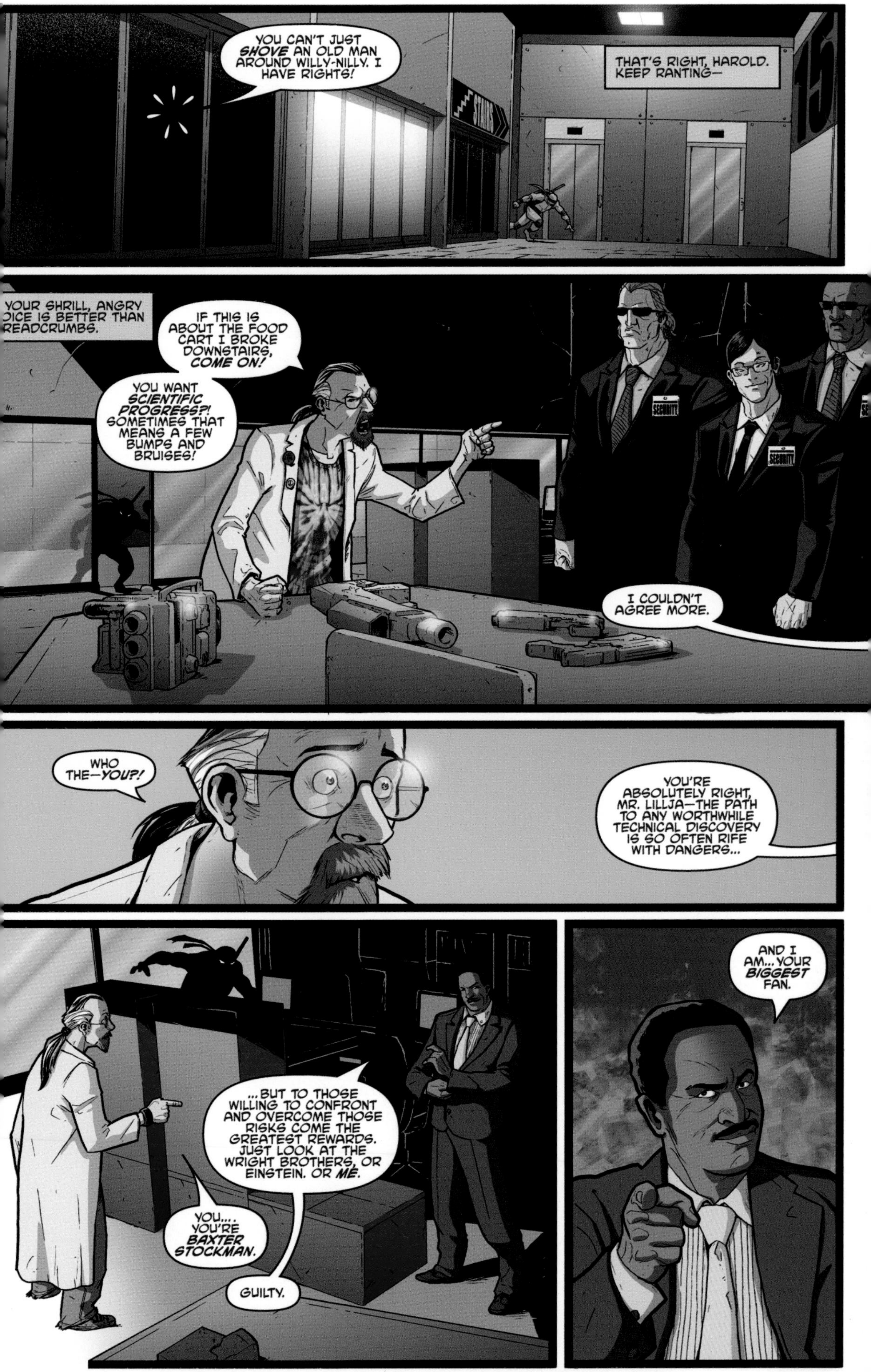
YOU CAN'T JUST SHOVE AN OLD MAN AROUND WILLY-NILLY. I HAVE RIGHTS!
THAT'S RIGHT, HAROLD. KEEP RANTING—
STAIRS
15
YOUR SHRILL, ANGRY OICE IS BETTER THAN READCRUMBS.
IF THIS IS ABOUT THE FOOD CART I BROKE DOWNSTAIRS, COME ON!
YOU WANT SCIENTIFIC PROGRESS?! SOMETIMES THAT MEANS A FEW BUMPS AND BRUISES!
SECURITY
SECURITY
I COULDN'T AGREE MORE.
WHO THE—YOU?!
YOU'RE ABSOLUTELY RIGHT, MR. LILLJA—THE PATH TO ANY WORTHWHILE TECHNICAL DISCOVERY IS SO OFTEN RIFE WITH DANGERS...
...BUT TO THOSE WILLING TO CONFRONT AND OVERCOME THOSE RISKS COME THE GREATEST REWARDS. JUST LOOK AT THE WRIGHT BROTHERS, OR EINSTEIN. OR ME.
YOU.... YOU'RE BAXTER STOCKMAN.
GUILTY.
AND I AM...YOUR BIGGEST FAN.

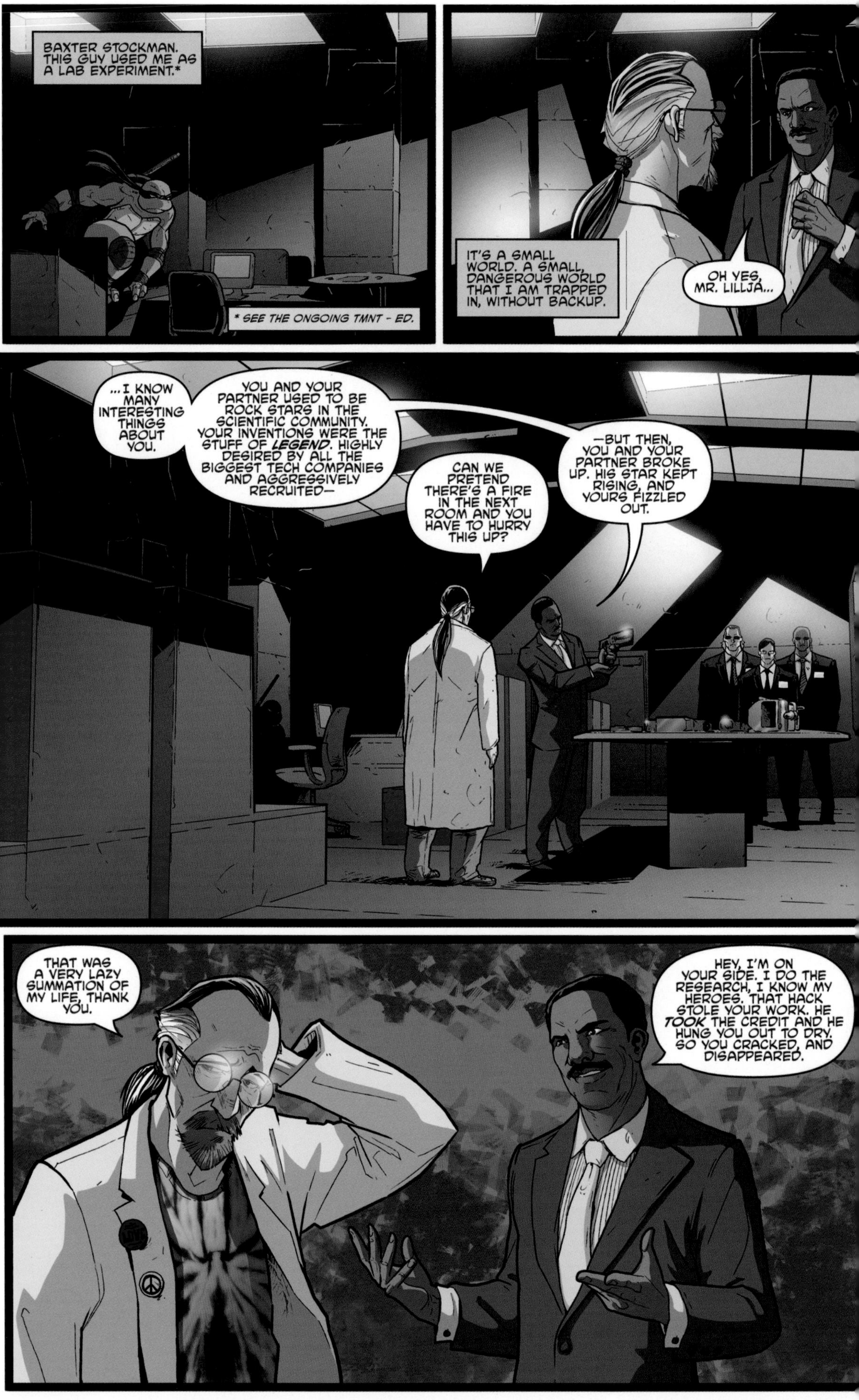
BAXTER STOCKMAN. THIS GUY USED ME AS A LAB EXPERIMENT.*
* SEE THE ONGOING TMNT - ED.
IT'S A SMALL WORLD. A SMALL, DANGEROUS WORLD THAT I AM TRAPPED IN, WITHOUT BACKUP.
OH YES, MR. LILLJA...
...I KNOW MANY INTERESTING THINGS ABOUT YOU.
YOU AND YOUR PARTNER USED TO BE ROCK STARS IN THE SCIENTIFIC COMMUNITY. YOUR INVENTIONS WERE THE STUFF OF LEGEND. HIGHLY DESIRED BY ALL THE BIGGEST TECH COMPANIES AND AGGRESSIVELY RECRUITED—
CAN WE PRETEND THERE'S A FIRE IN THE NEXT ROOM AND YOU HAVE TO HURRY THIS UP?
—BUT THEN, YOU AND YOUR PARTNER BROKE UP. HIS STAR KEPT RISING, AND YOURS FIZZLED OUT.
THAT WAS A VERY LAZY SUMMATION OF MY LIFE, THANK YOU.
HEY, I'M ON YOUR SIDE. I DO THE RESEARCH, I KNOW MY HEROES. THAT HACK STOLE YOUR WORK. HE TOOK THE CREDIT AND HE HUNG YOU OUT TO DRY. SO YOU CRACKED, AND DISAPPEARED.

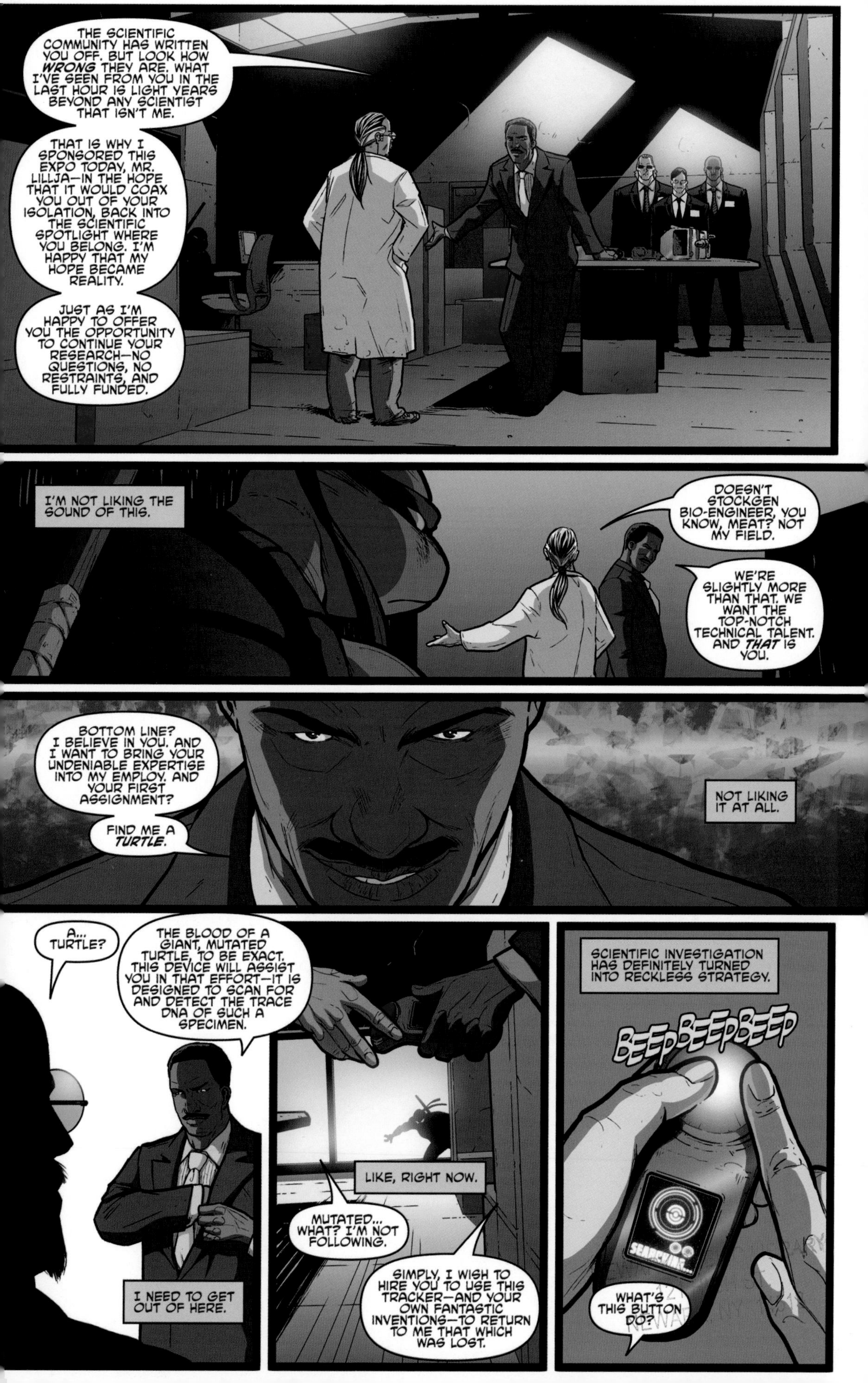
THE SCIENTIFIC COMMUNITY HAS WRITTEN YOU OFF. BUT LOOK HOW WRONG THEY ARE. WHAT I'VE SEEN FROM YOU IN THE LAST HOUR IS LIGHT YEARS BEYOND ANY SCIENTIST THAT ISN'T ME.
THAT IS WHY I SPONSORED THIS EXPO TODAY, MR. LILLJA—IN THE HOPE THAT IT WOULD COAX YOU OUT OF YOUR ISOLATION, BACK INTO THE SCIENTIFIC SPOTLIGHT WHERE YOU BELONG. I'M HAPPY THAT MY HOPE BECAME REALITY.
JUST AS I'M HAPPY TO OFFER YOU THE OPPORTUNITY TO CONTINUE YOUR RESEARCH—NO QUESTIONS, NO RESTRAINTS, AND FULLY FUNDED.
I'M NOT LIKING THE SOUND OF THIS.
DOESN'T STOCKGEN BIO-ENGINEER, YOU KNOW, MEAT? NOT MY FIELD.
WE'RE SLIGHTLY MORE THAN THAT. WE WANT THE TOP-NOTCH TECHNICAL TALENT. AND THAT IS YOU.
BOTTOM LINE? I BELIEVE IN YOU. AND I WANT TO BRING YOUR UNDENIABLE EXPERTISE INTO MY EMPLOY. AND YOUR FIRST ASSIGNMENT?
FIND ME A TURTLE.
NOT LIKING IT AT ALL.
A... TURTLE?
THE BLOOD OF A GIANT, MUTATED TURTLE, TO BE EXACT. THIS DEVICE WILL ASSIST YOU IN THAT EFFORT—IT IS DESIGNED TO SCAN FOR AND DETECT THE TRACE DNA OF SUCH A SPECIMEN.
I NEED TO GET OUT OF HERE.
LIKE, RIGHT NOW.
MUTATED... WHAT? I'M NOT FOLLOWING.
SIMPLY, I WISH TO HIRE YOU TO USE THIS TRACKER—AND YOUR OWN FANTASTIC INVENTIONS—TO RETURN TO ME THAT WHICH WAS LOST.
SCIENTIFIC INVESTIGATION HAS DEFINITELY TURNED INTO RECKLESS STRATEGY.
BEEPBEEPBEEP
SEARCHING...
WHAT'S THIS BUTTON DO?

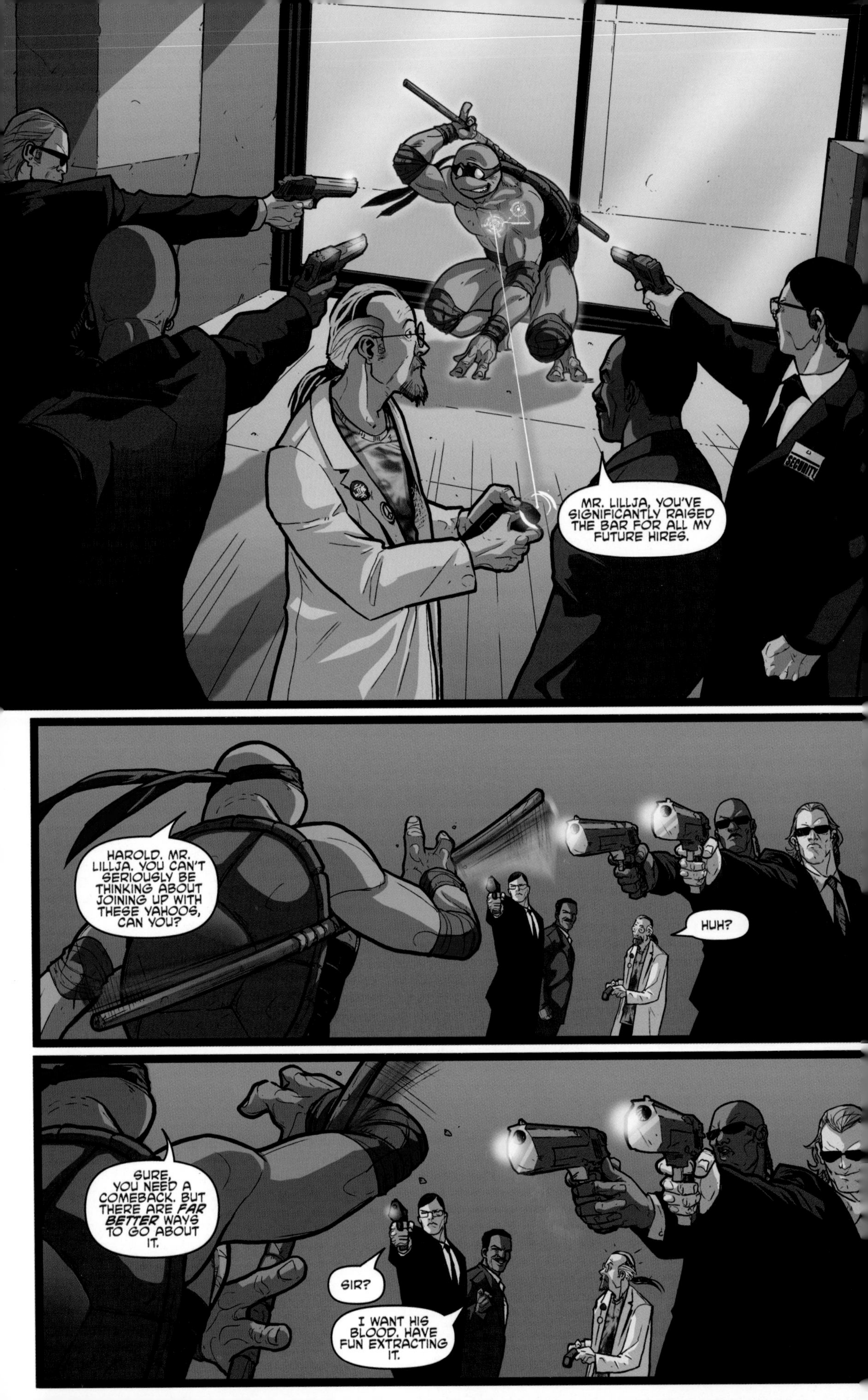
MR. LILLJA, YOU'VE SIGNIFICANTLY RAISED THE BAR FOR ALL MY FUTURE HIRES.
HAROLD. MR. LILLJA. YOU CAN'T SERIOUSLY BE THINKING ABOUT JOINING UP WITH THESE YAHOOS, CAN YOU?
HUH?
SURE, YOU NEED A COMEBACK. BUT THERE ARE *FAR BETTER* WAYS TO GO ABOUT IT.
SIR?
I WANT HIS BLOOD. HAVE FUN EXTRACTING IT.

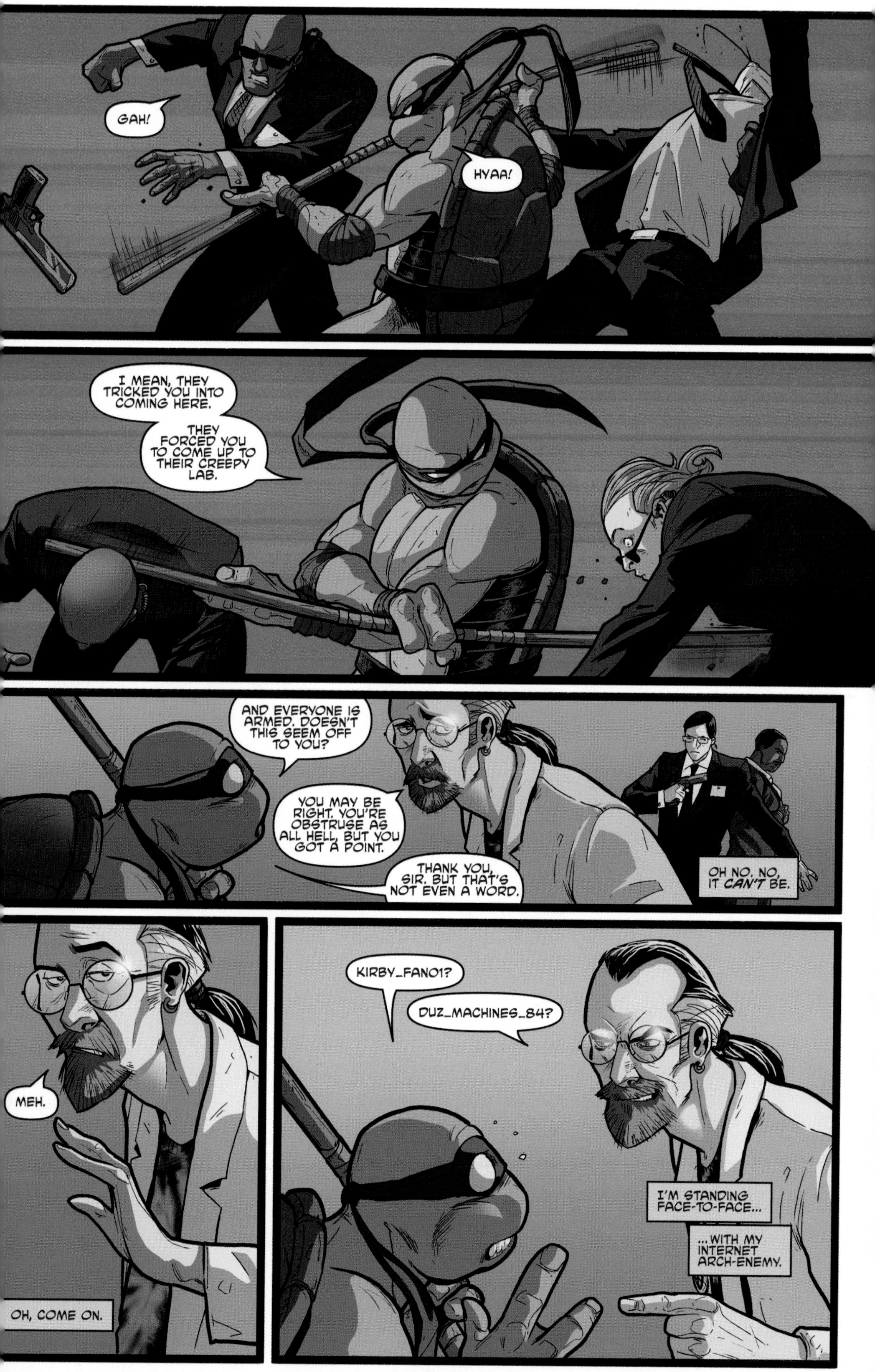
GAH!
HYAA!
I MEAN, THEY TRICKED YOU INTO COMING HERE.
THEY FORCED YOU TO COME UP TO THEIR CREEPY LAB.
AND EVERYONE IS ARMED. DOESN'T THIS SEEM OFF TO YOU?
YOU MAY BE RIGHT. YOU'RE OBSTRUSE AS ALL HELL, BUT YOU GOT A POINT.
THANK YOU, SIR. BUT THAT'S NOT EVEN A WORD.
OH NO. NO, IT *CAN'T* BE.
MEH.
OH, COME ON.
KIRBY_FAN01?
DUZ_MACHINES_84?
I'M STANDING FACE-TO-FACE...
...WITH MY INTERNET ARCH-ENEMY.

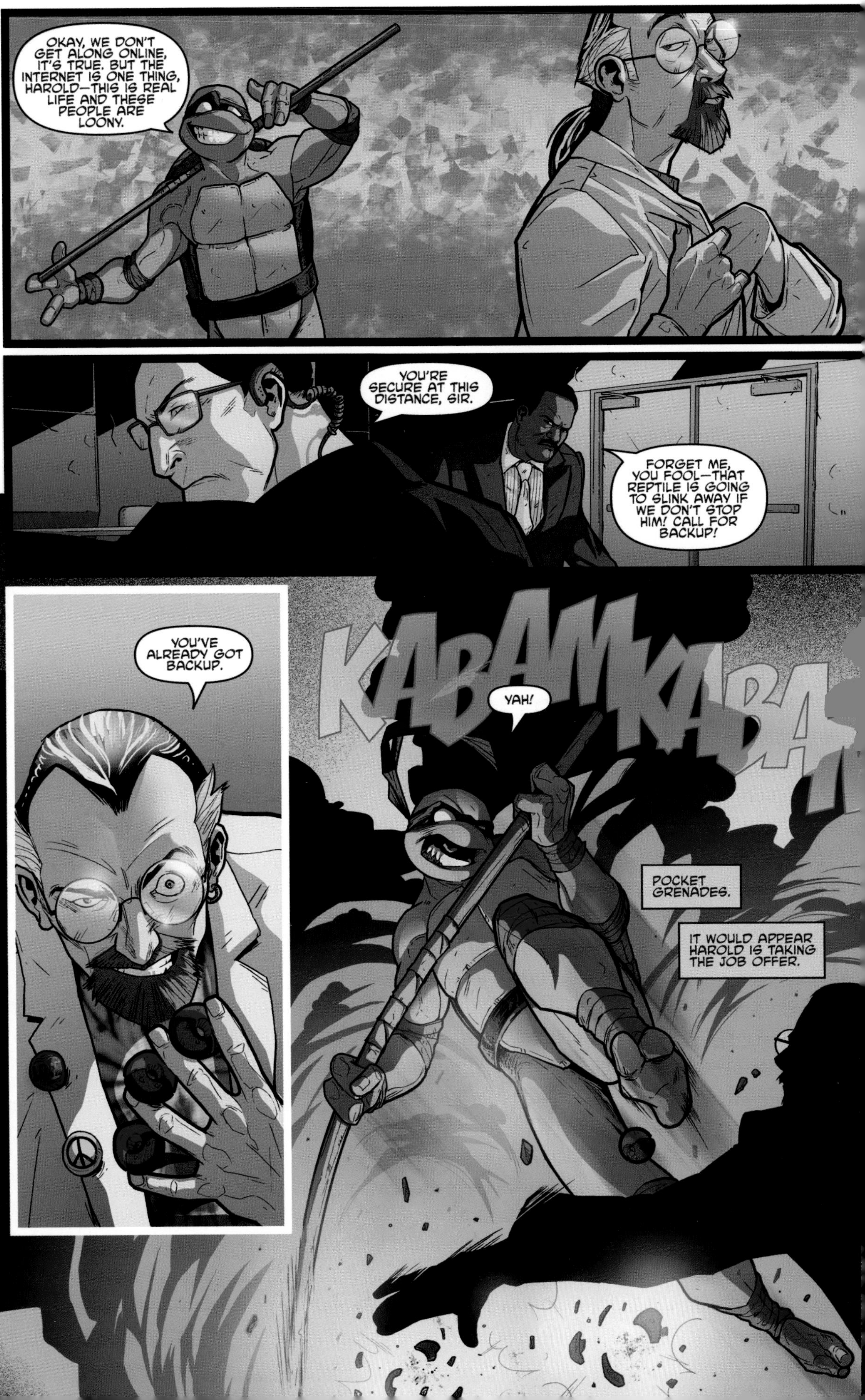
OKAY, WE DON'T GET ALONG ONLINE, IT'S TRUE. BUT THE INTERNET IS ONE THING, HAROLD—THIS IS REAL LIFE AND THESE PEOPLE ARE LOONY.
YOU'RE SECURE AT THIS DISTANCE, SIR.
FORGET ME, YOU FOOL—THAT REPTILE IS GOING TO SLINK AWAY IF WE DON'T STOP HIM! CALL FOR BACKUP!
YOU'VE ALREADY GOT BACKUP.
KABAMKABA
YAH!
POCKET GRENADES.
IT WOULD APPEAR HAROLD IS TAKING THE JOB OFFER.

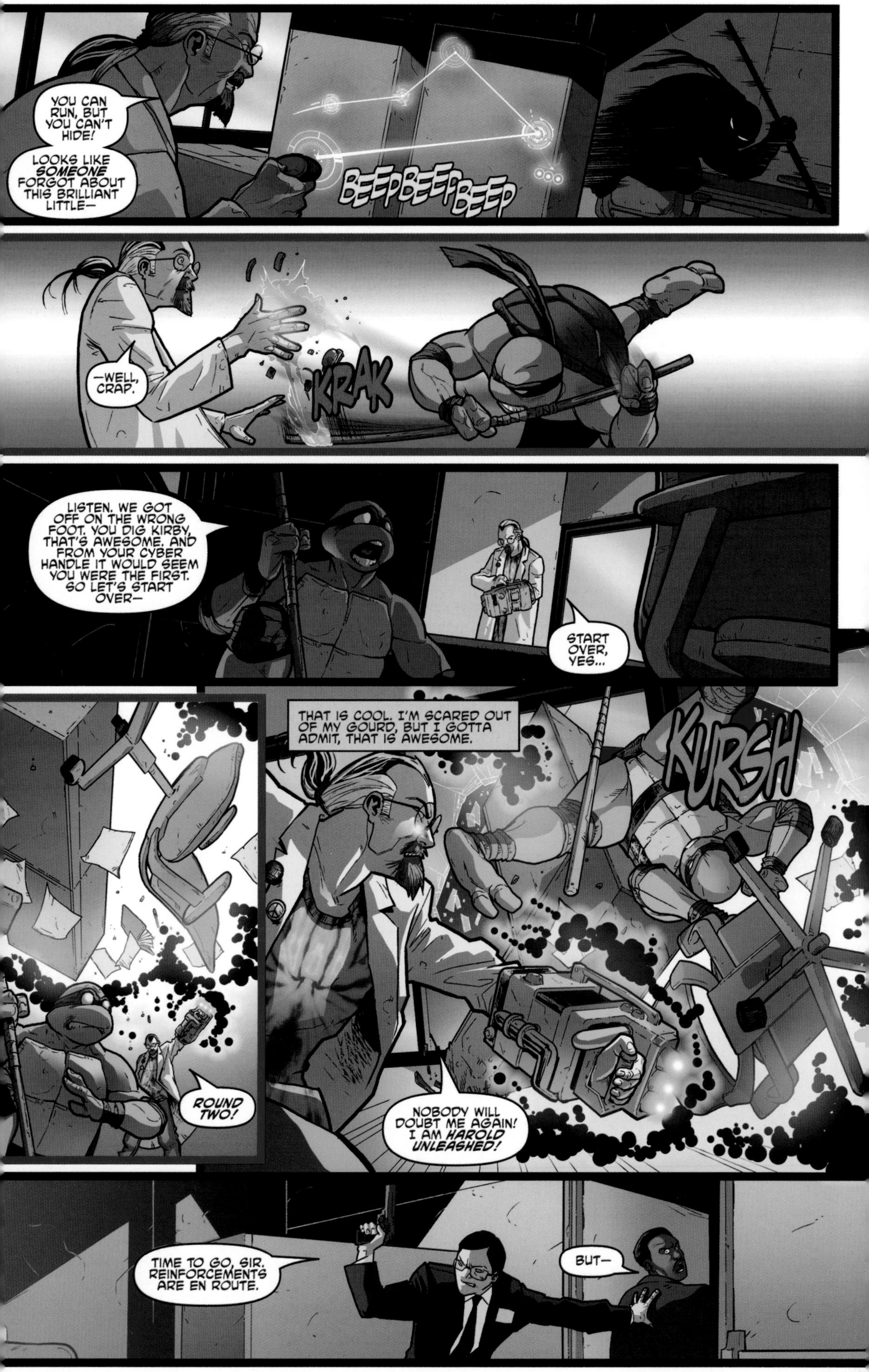
YOU CAN RUN, BUT YOU CAN'T HIDE!
LOOKS LIKE SOMEONE FORGOT ABOUT THIS BRILLIANT LITTLE—
BEEPBEEPBEEP
—WELL, CRAP.
KRAK
LISTEN. WE GOT OFF ON THE WRONG FOOT. YOU DIG KIRBY, THAT'S AWESOME. AND FROM YOUR CYBER HANDLE IT WOULD SEEM YOU WERE THE FIRST. SO LET'S START OVER—
START OVER, YES...
ROUND TWO!
THAT IS COOL. I'M SCARED OUT OF MY GOURD, BUT I GOTTA ADMIT, THAT IS AWESOME.
KURSH
NOBODY WILL DOUBT ME AGAIN! I AM HAROLD UNLEASHED!
TIME TO GO, SIR. REINFORCEMENTS ARE EN ROUTE.
BUT—

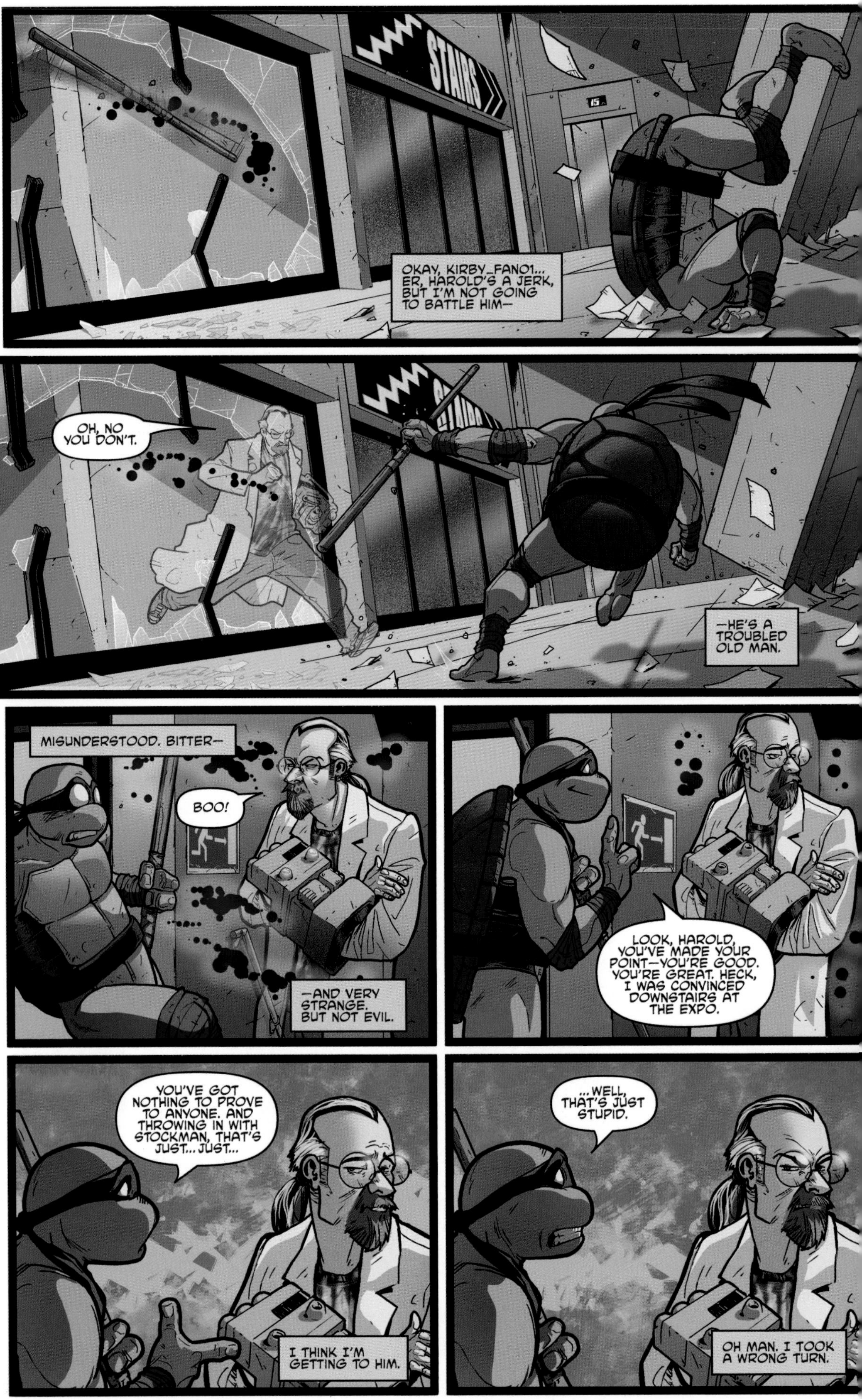
STAIRS
OKAY, KIRBY_FAN01... ER, HAROLD'S A JERK, BUT I'M NOT GOING TO BATTLE HIM—
OH, NO YOU DON'T.
—HE'S A TROUBLED OLD MAN.
MISUNDERSTOOD. BITTER—
BOO!
—AND VERY STRANGE. BUT NOT EVIL.
LOOK, HAROLD, YOU'VE MADE YOUR POINT—YOU'RE GOOD. YOU'RE GREAT. HECK, I WAS CONVINCED DOWNSTAIRS AT THE EXPO.
YOU'VE GOT NOTHING TO PROVE TO ANYONE. AND THROWING IN WITH STOCKMAN, THAT'S JUST... JUST...
I THINK I'M GETTING TO HIM.
...WELL, THAT'S JUST STUPID.
OH MAN. I TOOK A WRONG TURN.

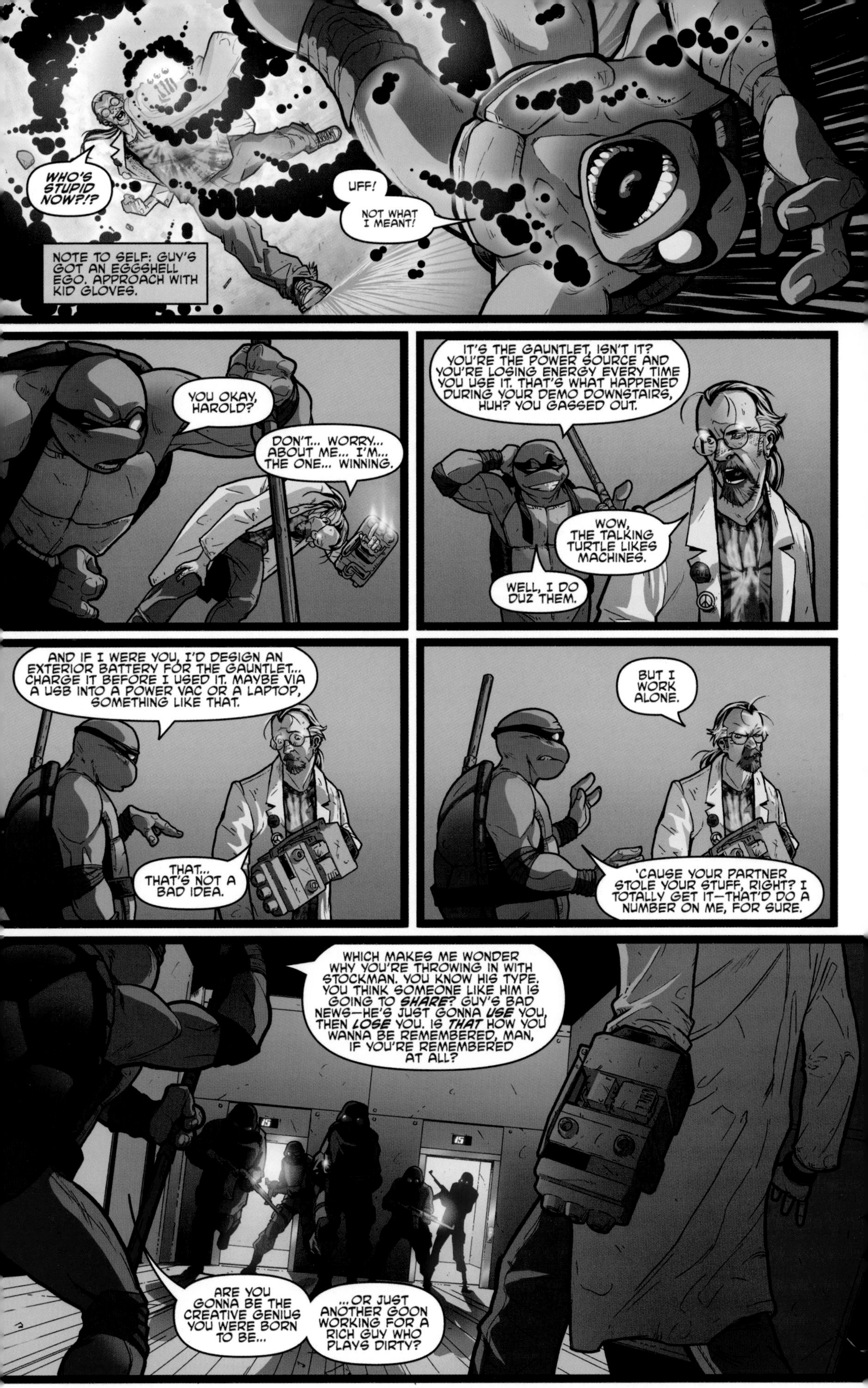
WHO'S STUPID NOW?!?
UFF!
NOT WHAT I MEANT!
NOTE TO SELF: GUY'S GOT AN EGGSHELL EGO. APPROACH WITH KID GLOVES.
YOU OKAY, HAROLD?
DON'T... WORRY... ABOUT ME... I'M... THE ONE... WINNING.
IT'S THE GAUNTLET, ISN'T IT? YOU'RE THE POWER SOURCE AND YOU'RE LOSING ENERGY EVERY TIME YOU USE IT. THAT'S WHAT HAPPENED DURING YOUR DEMO DOWNSTAIRS, HUH? YOU GASSED OUT.
WOW, THE TALKING TURTLE LIKES MACHINES.
WELL, I DO DUZ THEM.
AND IF I WERE YOU, I'D DESIGN AN EXTERIOR BATTERY FOR THE GAUNTLET... CHARGE IT BEFORE I USED IT. MAYBE VIA A USB INTO A POWER VAC OR A LAPTOP, SOMETHING LIKE THAT.
THAT... THAT'S NOT A BAD IDEA.
BUT I WORK ALONE.
'CAUSE YOUR PARTNER STOLE YOUR STUFF, RIGHT? I TOTALLY GET IT—THAT'D DO A NUMBER ON ME, FOR SURE.
WHICH MAKES ME WONDER WHY YOU'RE THROWING IN WITH STOCKMAN. YOU KNOW HIS TYPE. YOU THINK SOMEONE LIKE HIM IS GOING TO SHARE? GUY'S BAD NEWS—HE'S JUST GONNA USE YOU, THEN LOSE YOU. IS THAT HOW YOU WANNA BE REMEMBERED, MAN, IF YOU'RE REMEMBERED AT ALL?
ARE YOU GONNA BE THE CREATIVE GENIUS YOU WERE BORN TO BE...
...OR JUST ANOTHER GOON WORKING FOR A RICH GUY WHO PLAYS DIRTY?

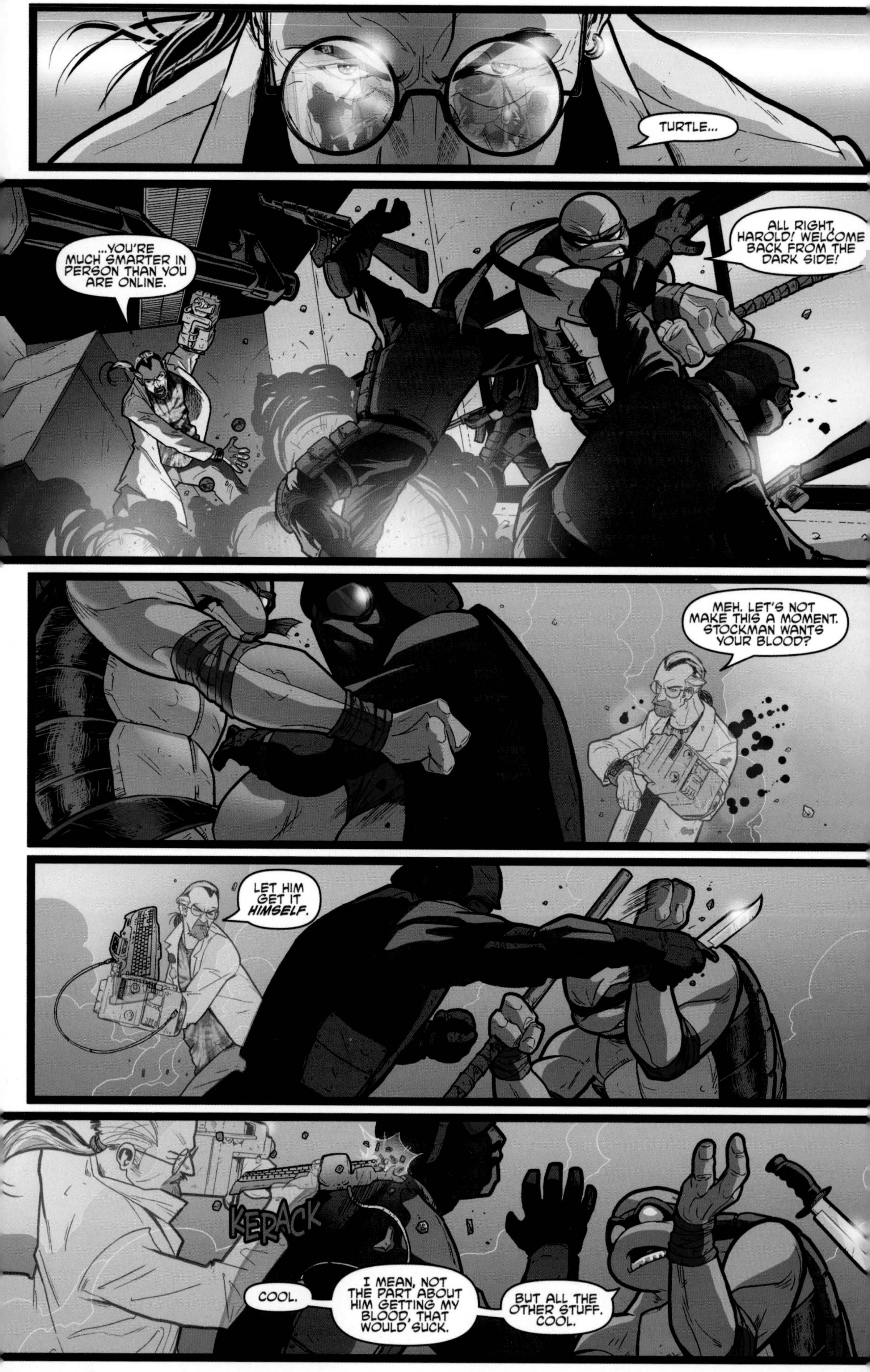
TURTLE...
...YOU'RE MUCH SMARTER IN PERSON THAN YOU ARE ONLINE.
ALL RIGHT, HAROLD! WELCOME BACK FROM THE DARK SIDE!
MEH. LET'S NOT MAKE THIS A MOMENT. STOCKMAN WANTS YOUR BLOOD?
LET HIM GET IT HIMSELF.
KERACK
COOL.
I MEAN, NOT THE PART ABOUT HIM GETTING MY BLOOD, THAT WOULD SUCK.
BUT ALL THE OTHER STUFF. COOL.

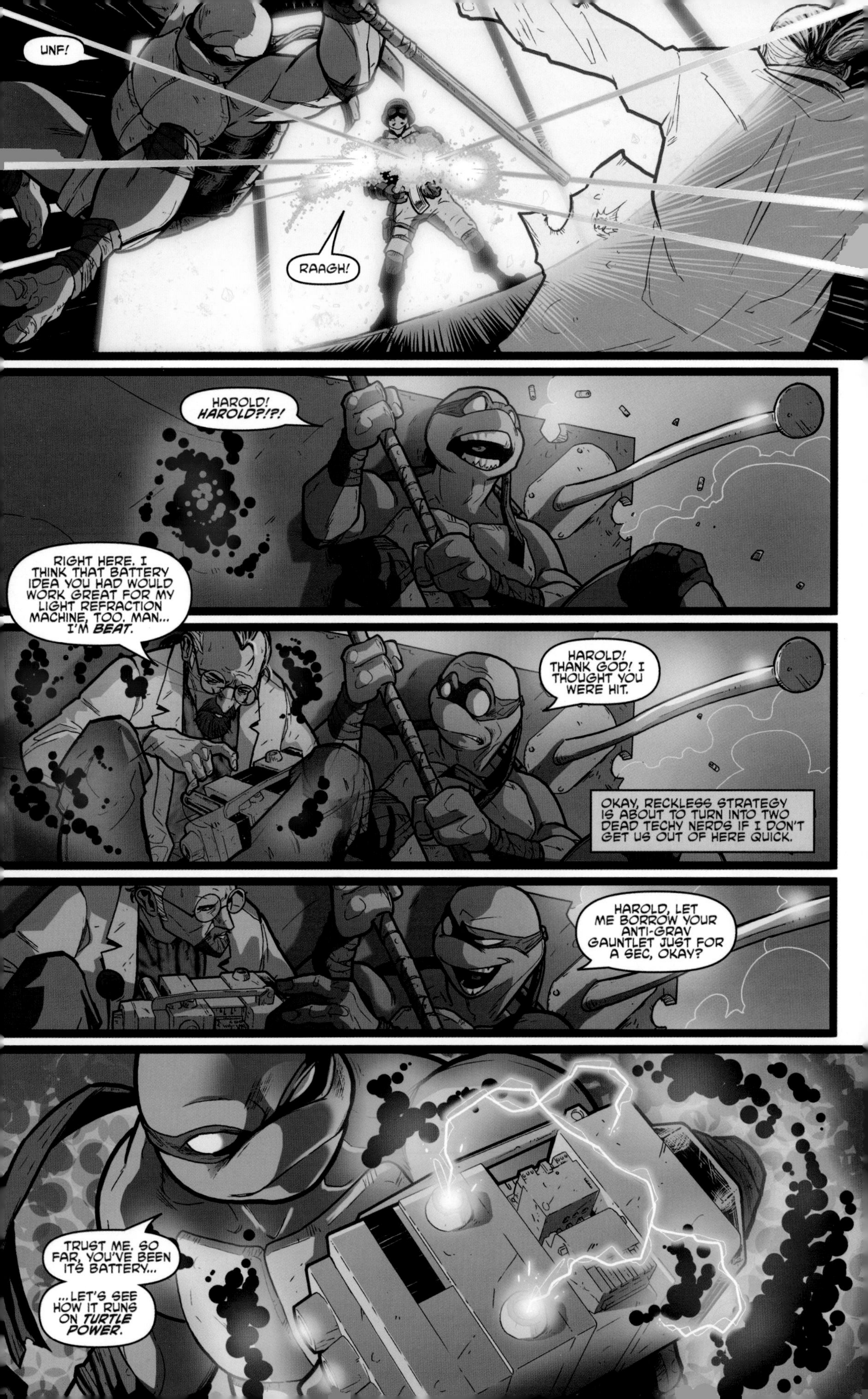
UNF!
RAAGH!
HAROLD! HAROLD?!?!
RIGHT HERE. I THINK THAT BATTERY IDEA YOU HAD WOULD WORK GREAT FOR MY LIGHT REFRACTION MACHINE, TOO. MAN... I'M BEAT.
HAROLD! THANK GOD! I THOUGHT YOU WERE HIT.
OKAY, RECKLESS STRATEGY IS ABOUT TO TURN INTO TWO DEAD TECHY NERDS IF I DON'T GET US OUT OF HERE QUICK.
HAROLD, LET ME BORROW YOUR ANTI-GRAV GAUNTLET JUST FOR A SEC, OKAY?
TRUST ME. SO FAR, YOU'VE BEEN ITS BATTERY...
...LET'S SEE HOW IT RUNS ON TURTLE POWER.

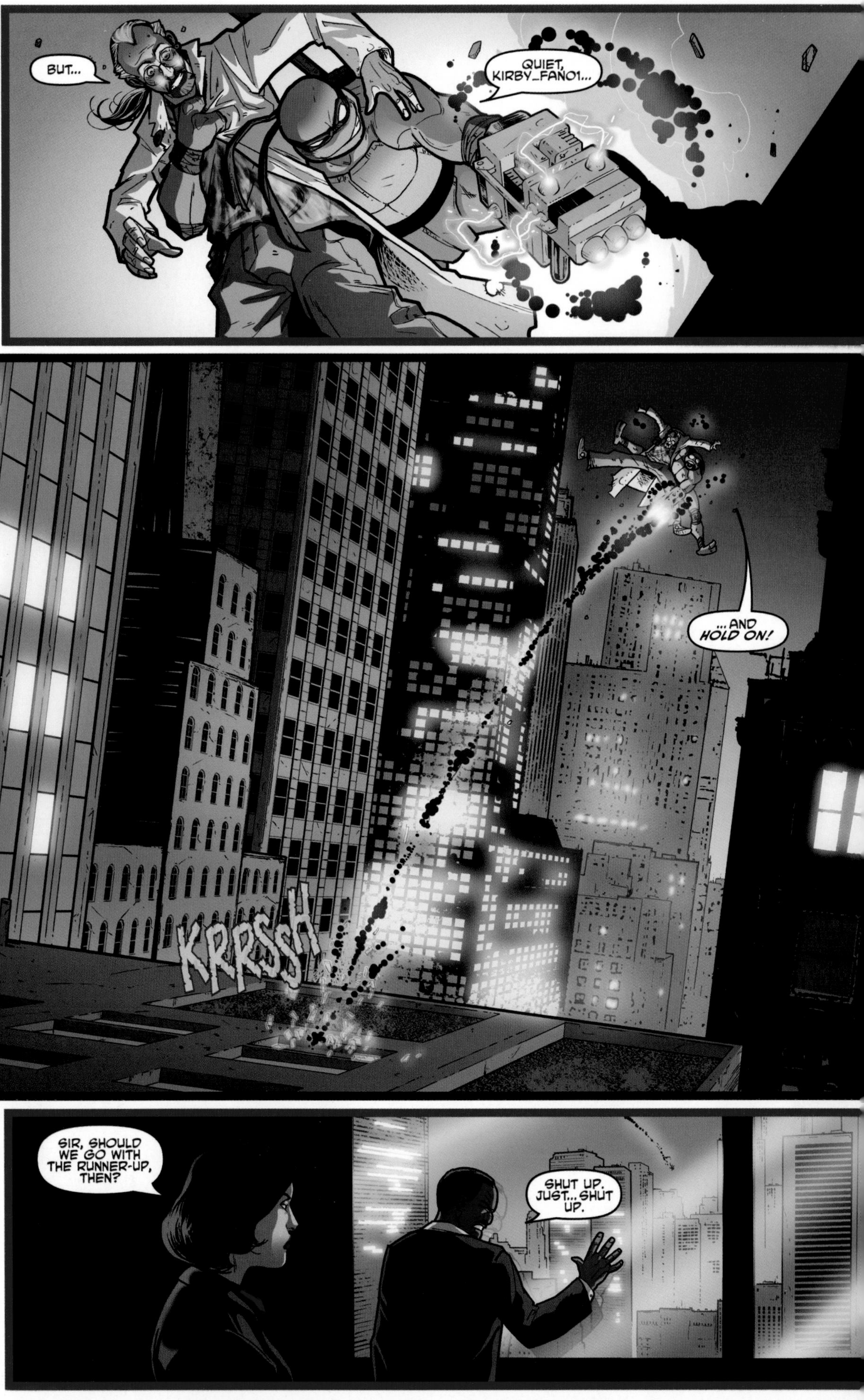
BUT...
QUIET, KIRBY_FAN01...
...AND HOLD ON!
KRRSSH
SIR, SHOULD WE GO WITH THE RUNNER-UP, THEN?
SHUT UP. JUST... SHUT UP.

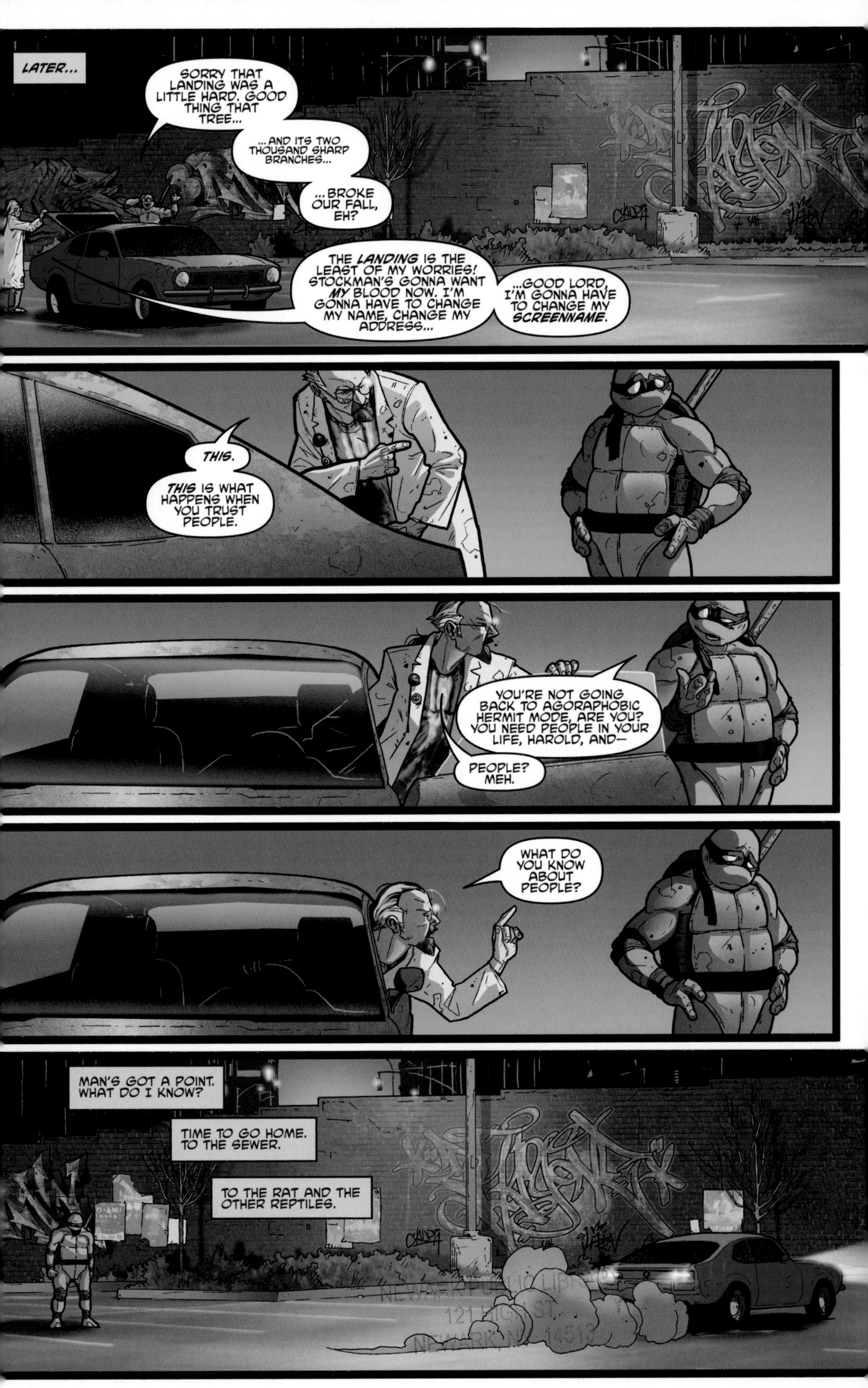
LATER...
SORRY THAT LANDING WAS A LITTLE HARD. GOOD THING THAT TREE...
...AND ITS TWO THOUSAND SHARP BRANCHES...
...BROKE OUR FALL, EH?
THE LANDING IS THE LEAST OF MY WORRIES! STOCKMAN'S GONNA WANT MY BLOOD NOW. I'M GONNA HAVE TO CHANGE MY NAME, CHANGE MY ADDRESS...
...GOOD LORD, I'M GONNA HAVE TO CHANGE MY SCREENNAME.
THIS.
THIS IS WHAT HAPPENS WHEN YOU TRUST PEOPLE.
YOU'RE NOT GOING BACK TO AGORAPHOBIC HERMIT MODE, ARE YOU? YOU NEED PEOPLE IN YOUR LIFE, HAROLD, AND—
PEOPLE? MEH.
WHAT DO YOU KNOW ABOUT PEOPLE?
MAN'S GOT A POINT. WHAT DO I KNOW?
TIME TO GO HOME. TO THE SEWER.
TO THE RAT AND THE OTHER REPTILES.

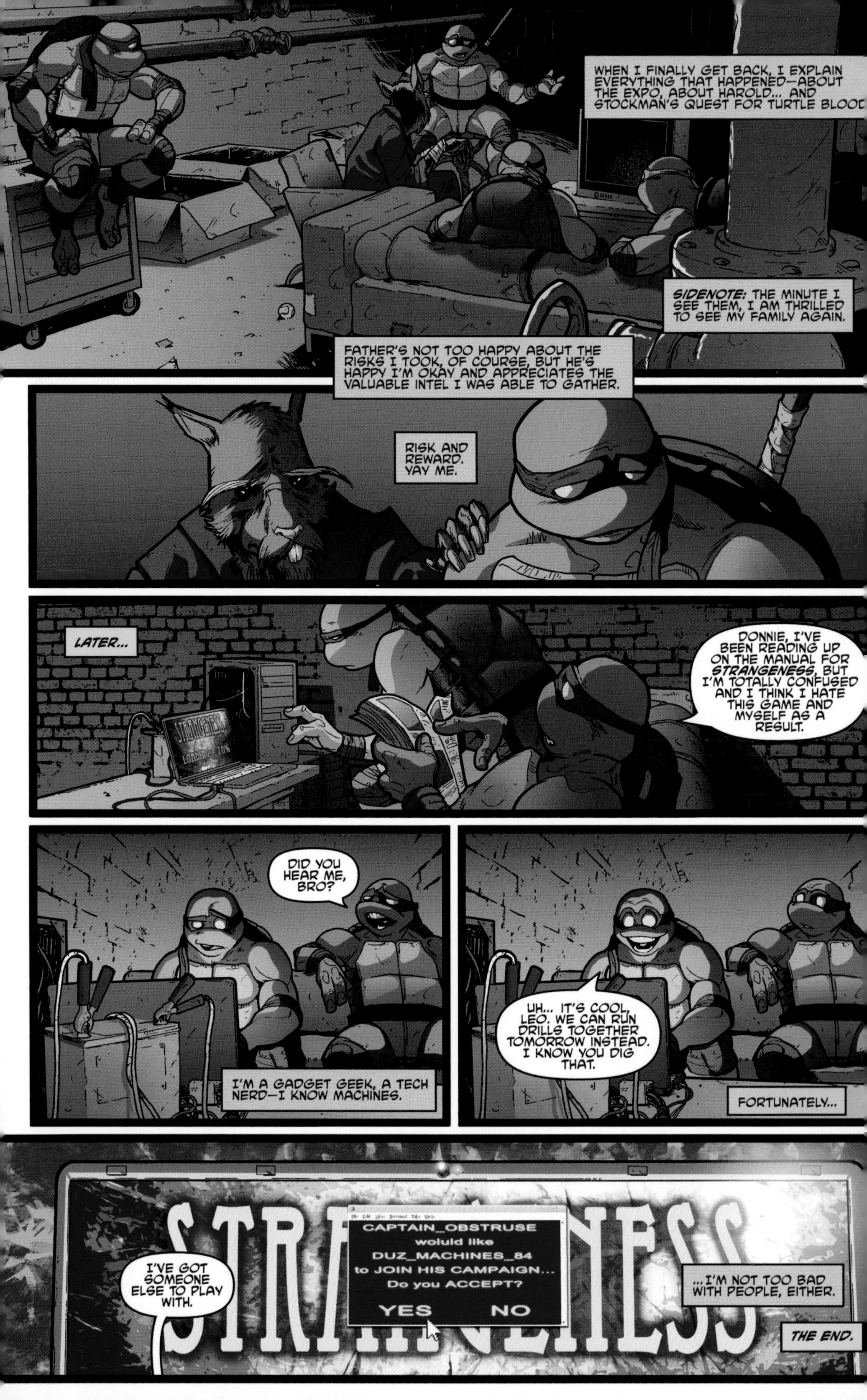
WHEN I FINALLY GET BACK, I EXPLAIN EVERYTHING THAT HAPPENED—ABOUT THE EXPO, ABOUT HAROLD... AND STOCKMAN'S QUEST FOR TURTLE BLOOD
SIDENOTE: THE MINUTE I SEE THEM, I AM THRILLED TO SEE MY FAMILY AGAIN.
FATHER'S NOT TOO HAPPY ABOUT THE RISKS I TOOK, OF COURSE, BUT HE'S HAPPY I'M OKAY AND APPRECIATES THE VALUABLE INTEL I WAS ABLE TO GATHER.
RISK AND REWARD. YAY ME.
LATER...
DONNIE, I'VE BEEN READING UP ON THE MANUAL FOR STRANGENESS, BUT I'M TOTALLY CONFUSED AND I THINK I HATE THIS GAME AND MYSELF AS A RESULT.
DID YOU HEAR ME, BRO?
I'M A GADGET GEEK, A TECH NERD—I KNOW MACHINES.
UH... IT'S COOL, LEO. WE CAN RUN DRILLS TOGETHER TOMORROW INSTEAD. I KNOW YOU DIG THAT.
FORTUNATELY...
CAPTAIN_OBSTRUSE woluld like DUZ_MACHINES_84 to JOIN HIS CAMPAIGN... Do you ACCEPT?
YES NO
I'VE GOT SOMEONE ELSE TO PLAY WITH.
...I'M NOT TOO BAD WITH PEOPLE, EITHER.
THE END.